The Frog and the Ox

Can bragging get you into trouble?

www.av2books.com

Go to www.av2books.com, and enter this book's unique code.

BOOK CODE

F311692

AV² **by Weigl** brings you media enhanced books that support active learning.

Published by AV² by Weigl
350 5th Avenue, 59th Floor New York, NY 10118

Copyright ©2013 AV² by Weigl
Copyright ©2010 by Kyowon Co., Ltd.

Library of Congress Cataloging-in-Publication Data

The frog and the ox.
    p. cm. -- (Aesop's fables by AV2)
  Summary: The classic Aesop fable is performed by a troupe of animal actors.
  ISBN 978-1-61913-104-0 (hard cover : alk. paper)
  [1. Fables. 2. Folklore.] I. Aesop.
  PZ8.2.F8 2012
  398.2--dc23
  [E]
                            2012018613

Printed in the United States in North Mankato, Minnesota
1 2 3 4 5 6 7 8 9 0 16 15 14 13 12

052012
WEP110612

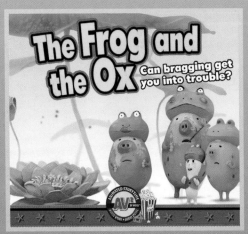

FABLE SYNOPSIS

For thousands of years, parents and teachers have used memorable stories called fables to teach simple moral lessons to children.

In the Aesop's Fables by AV² series, classic fables are given a lighthearted twist. These familiar tales are performed by a troupe of animal players whose endearing personalities bring the stories to life.

In *The Frog and the Ox,* Aesop and his troupe teach their audience to be careful of being overconfident. Aesop learns the hard way that bragging may get you into trouble.

This AV² media enhanced book comes alive with...

Animated Video
Watch a custom animated movie.

Try This!
Complete activities and hands on experiments.

Key Words
Study vocabulary and hands-on experiments.

Quiz
Test your knowledge.

The Frog and the Ox

Can bragging get you into trouble?

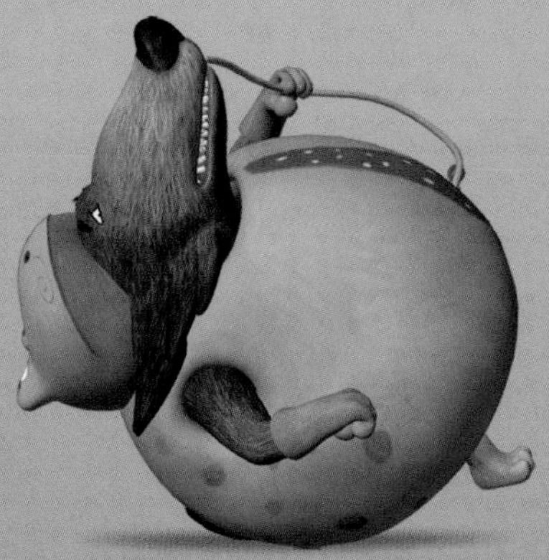

AV² Storytime Navigation

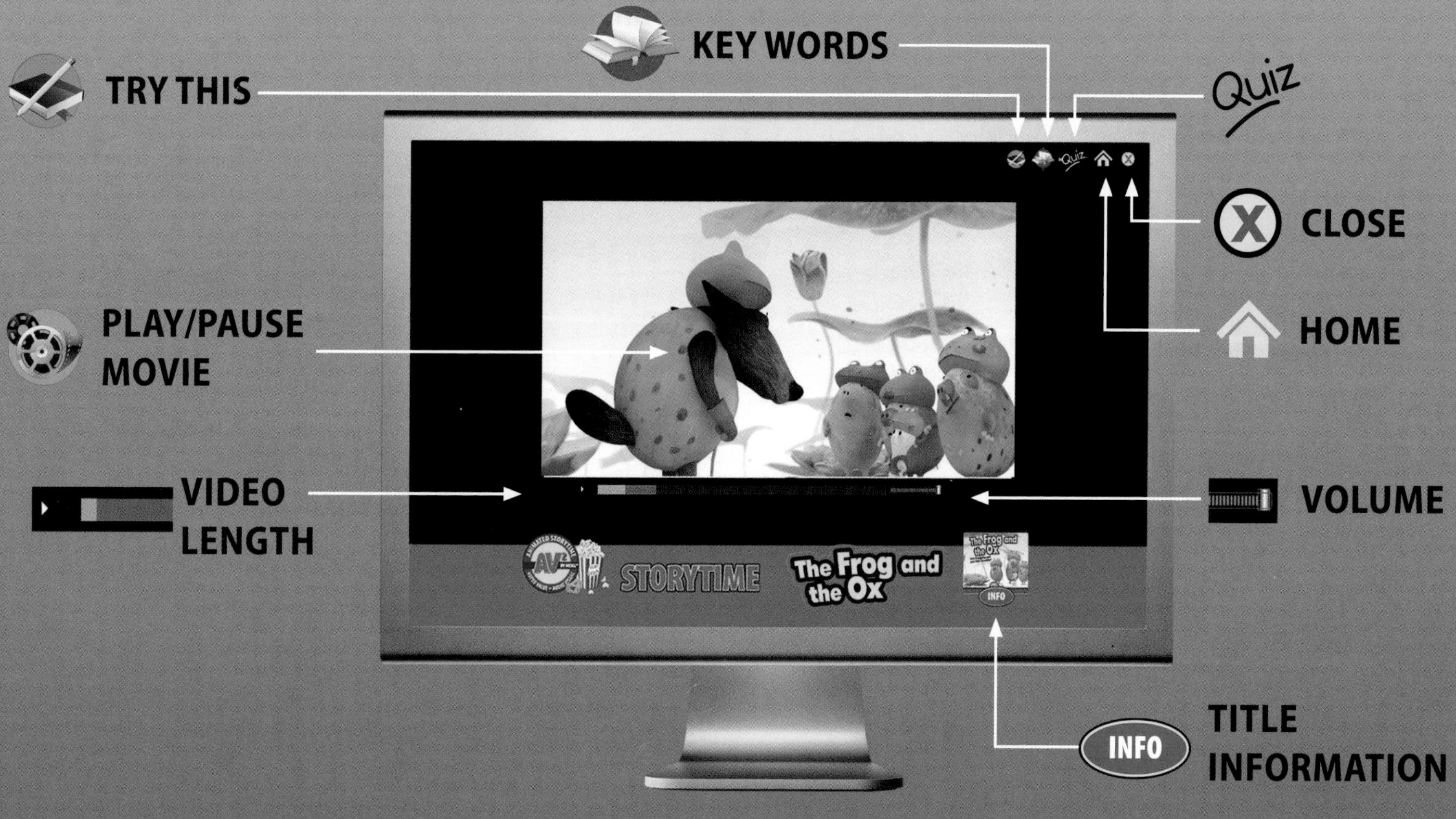
KEY WORDS
TRY THIS
Quiz
CLOSE
HOME
PLAY/PAUSE MOVIE
VIDEO LENGTH
VOLUME
STORYTIME
The Frog and the Ox
INFO
TITLE INFORMATION

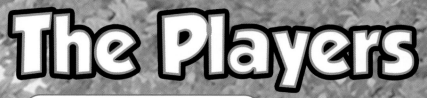

The Players

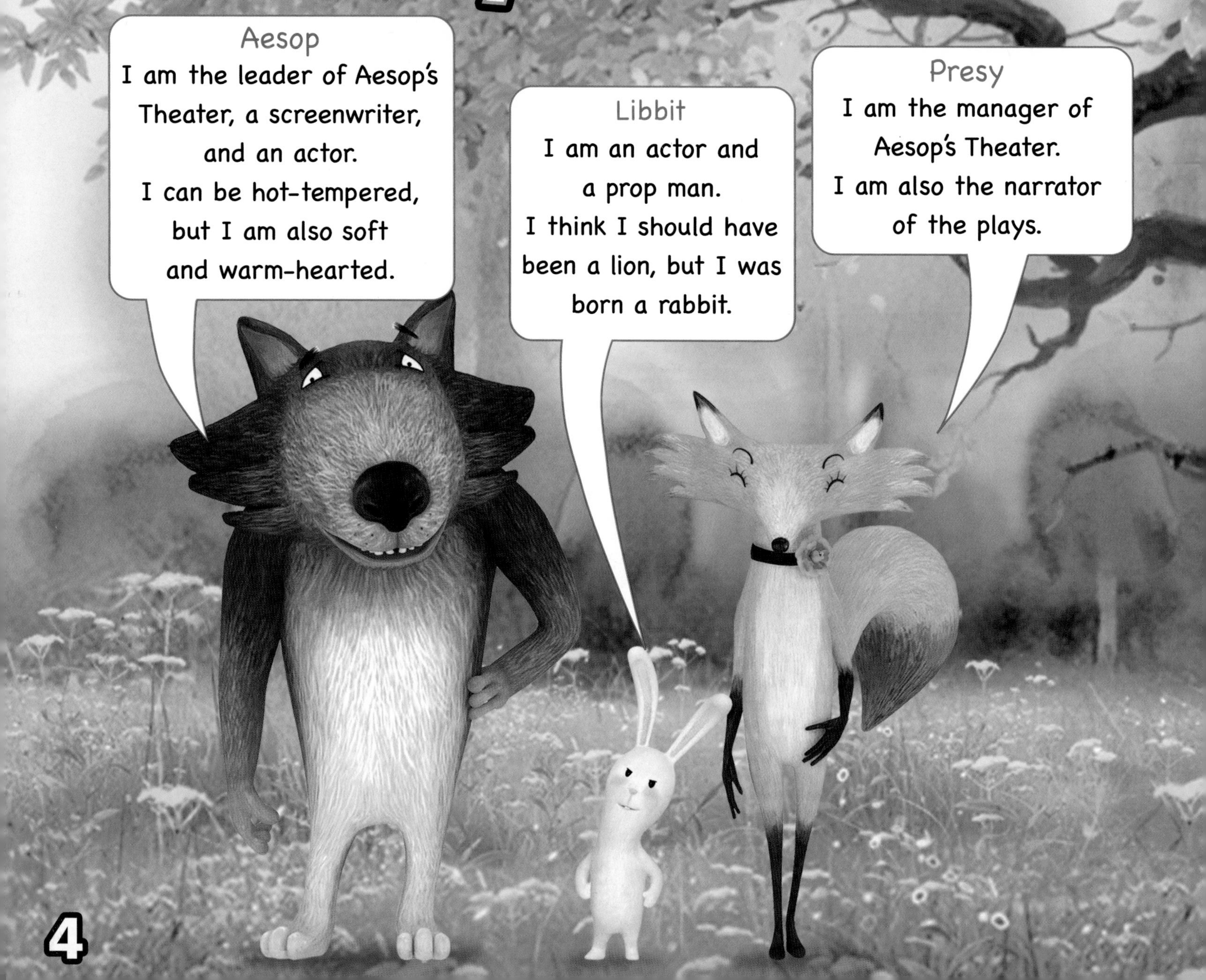
Aesop
I am the leader of Aesop's Theater, a screenwriter, and an actor. I can be hot-tempered, but I am also soft and warm-hearted.
Libbit
I am an actor and a prop man. I think I should have been a lion, but I was born a rabbit.
Presy
I am the manager of Aesop's Theater. I am also the narrator of the plays.

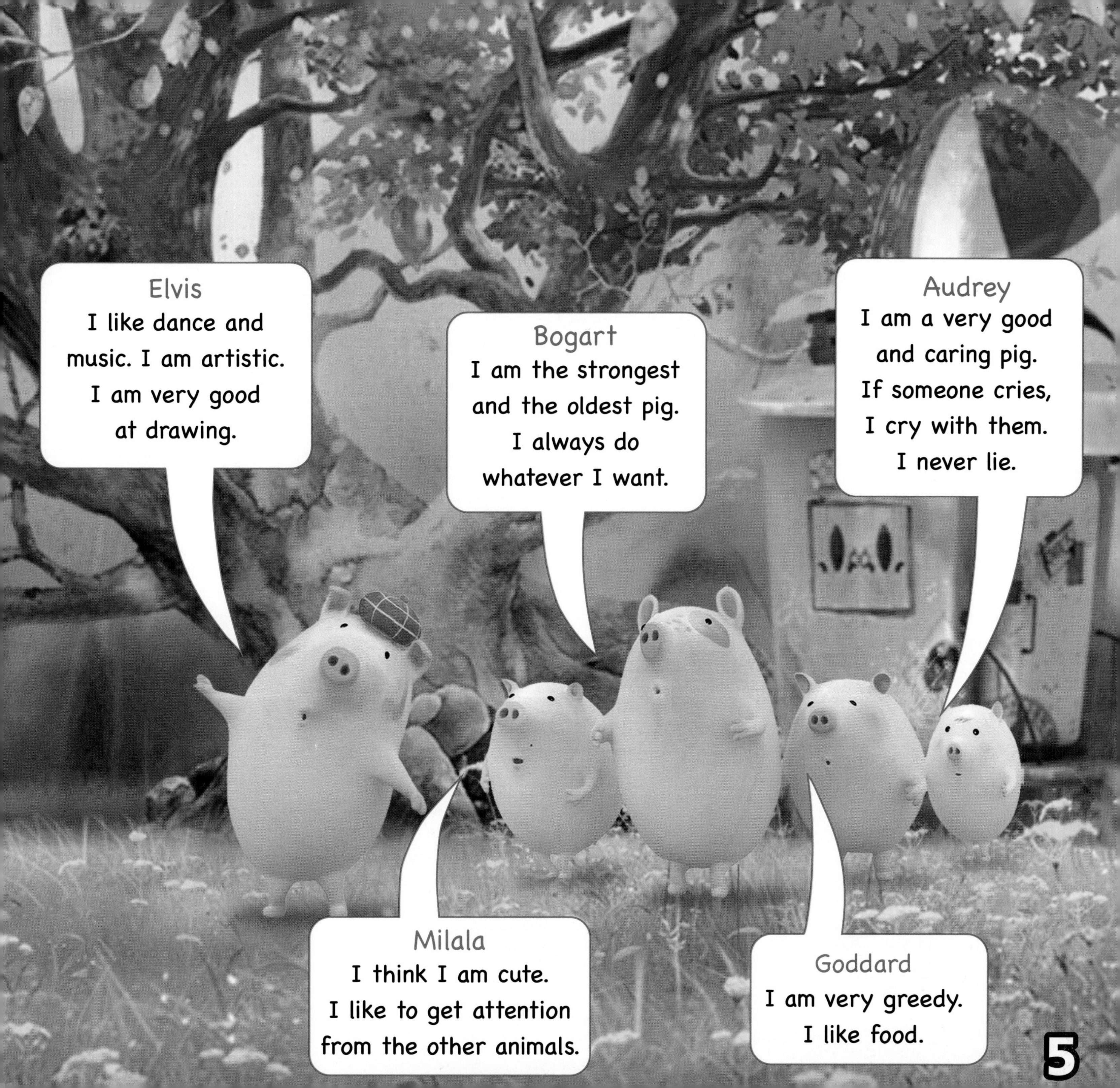
Elvis I like dance and music. I am artistic. I am very good at drawing.
Bogart I am the strongest and the oldest pig. I always do whatever I want.
Audrey I am a very good and caring pig. If someone cries, I cry with them. I never lie.
Milala I think I am cute. I like to get attention from the other animals.
Goddard I am very greedy. I like food.

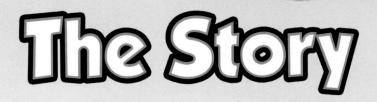

The Story

One morning, near a large pond, six young frogs were singing happily with their father. "Ribbit! Ribbit!"

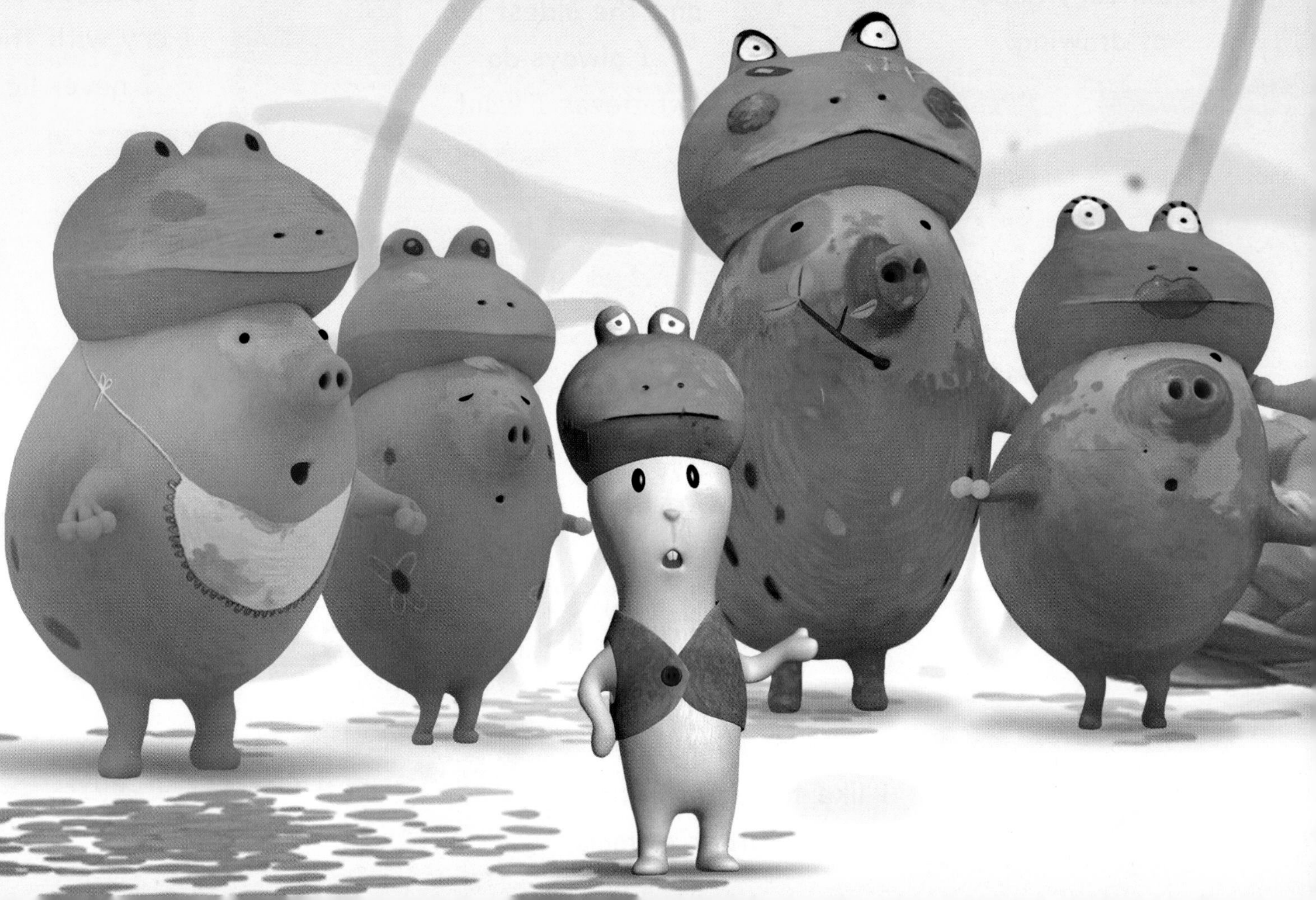

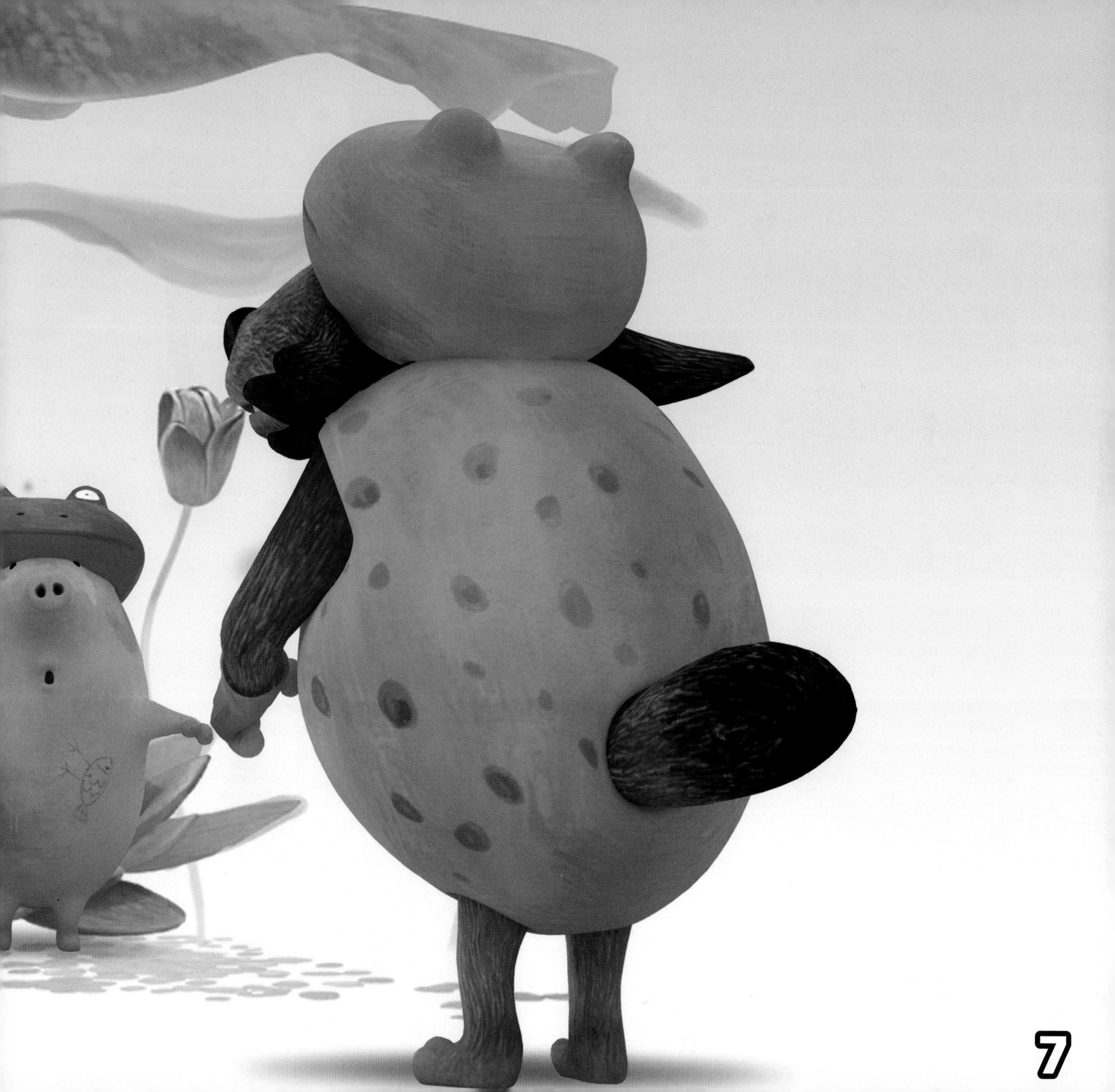

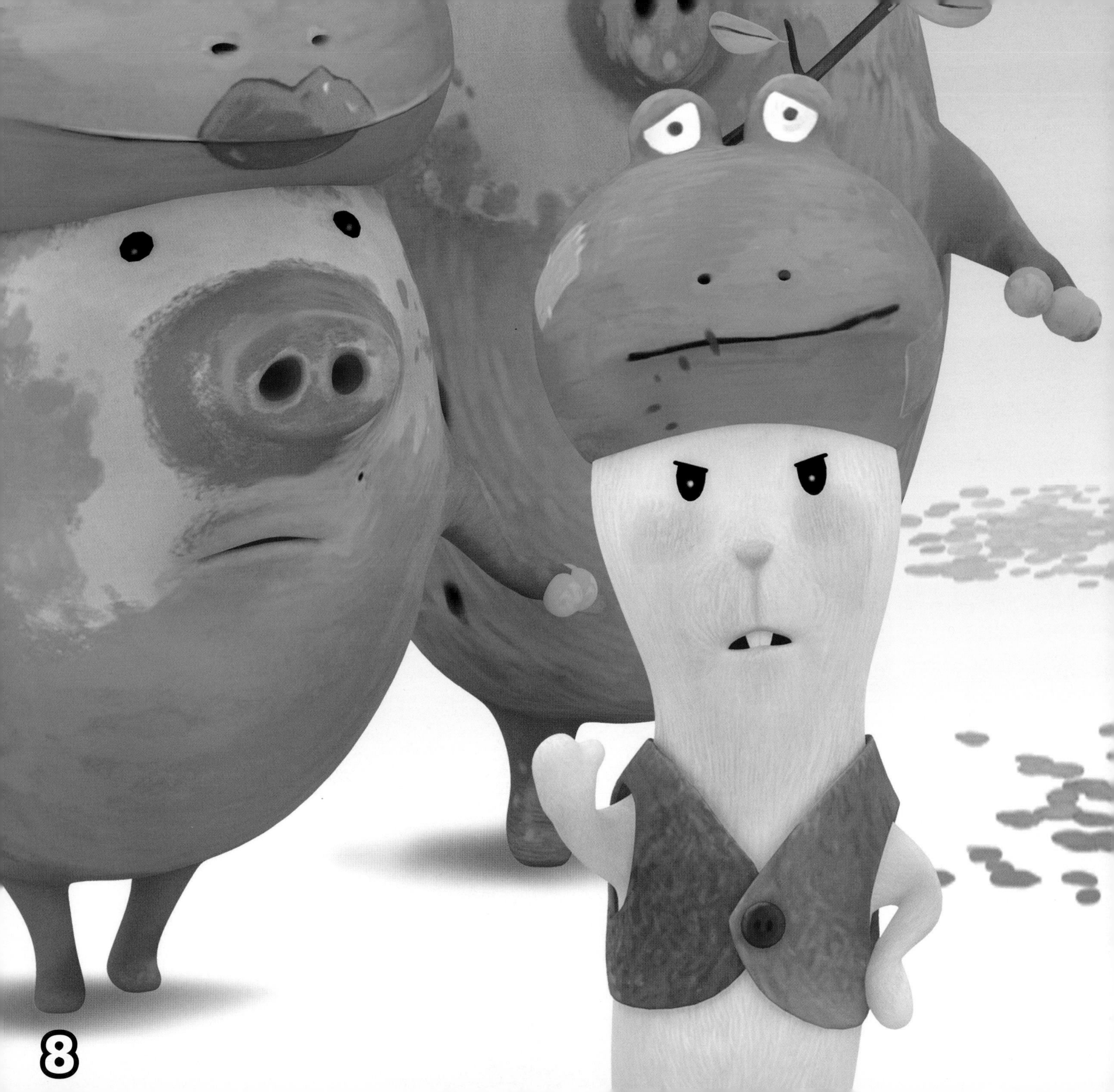

The little frog said,

"Daddy, I just saw a big monster!"

The little frog spread his arms out wide.

"He was very big. He had horns on his head,

and his tail was long.

He looked scary."

The father frog smiled.

"My child, he's not a monster, he's an ox."

"Ox?" The little frog had never seen an ox before.

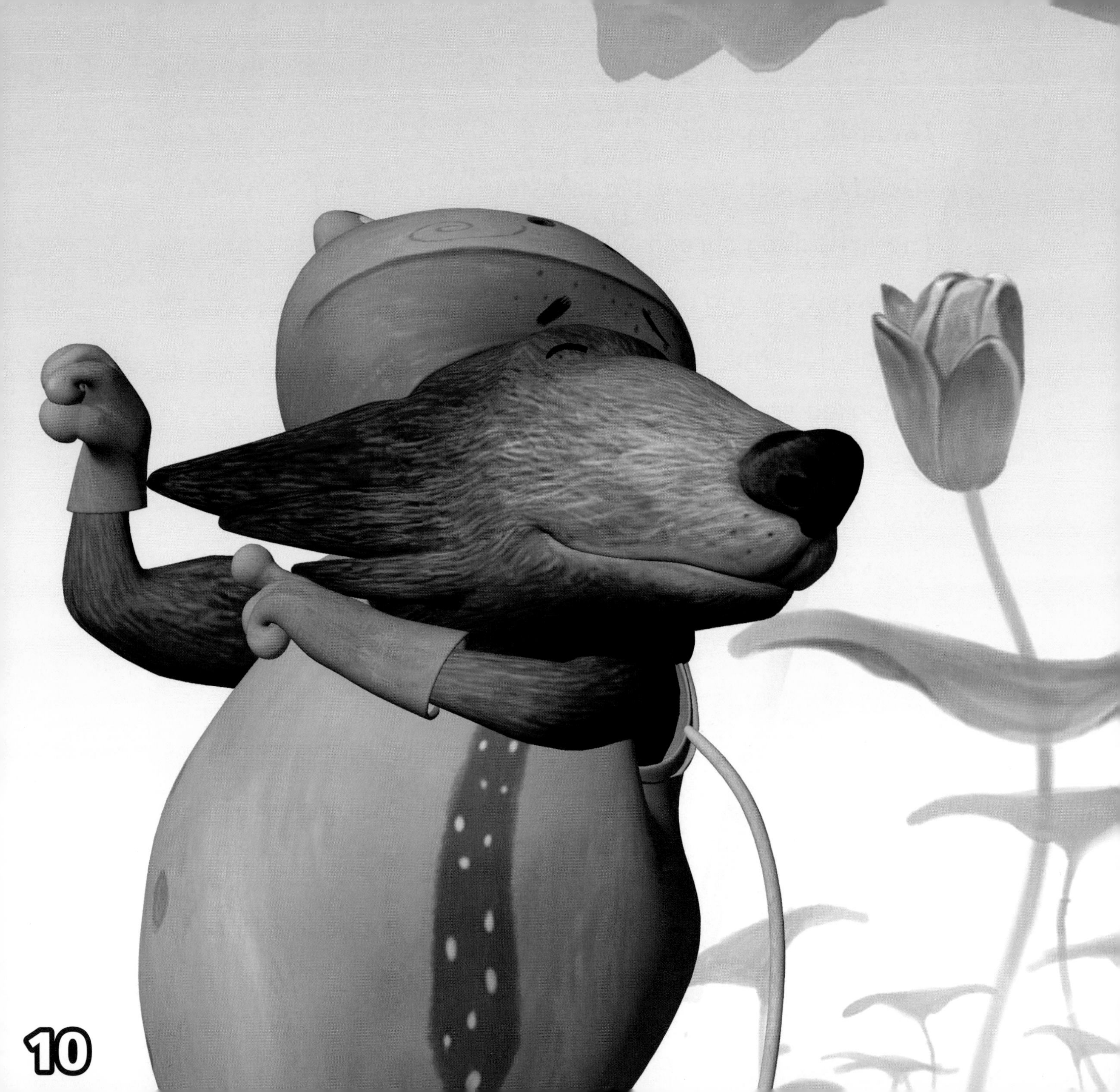

The father frog began puffing air into his chest.

"Don't worry, I can make myself as big as the ox."

Then, the father frog swelled right up.

"Was the ox as big as me?"

"The ox was much bigger," said the little frog.

The father frog puffed up again.

"Was the ox as big as I am now?"

The little frog said, "He was even bigger."

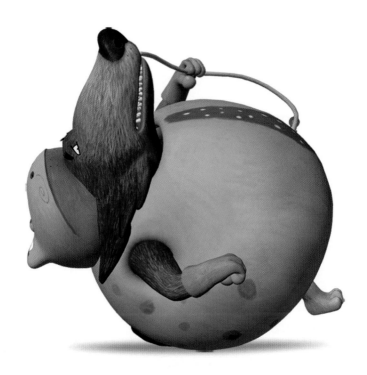

The father frog managed to puff up again.

"Was the ox bigger than I am now?"

The little frog nodded his head.

The father frog squeezed in one last puff.

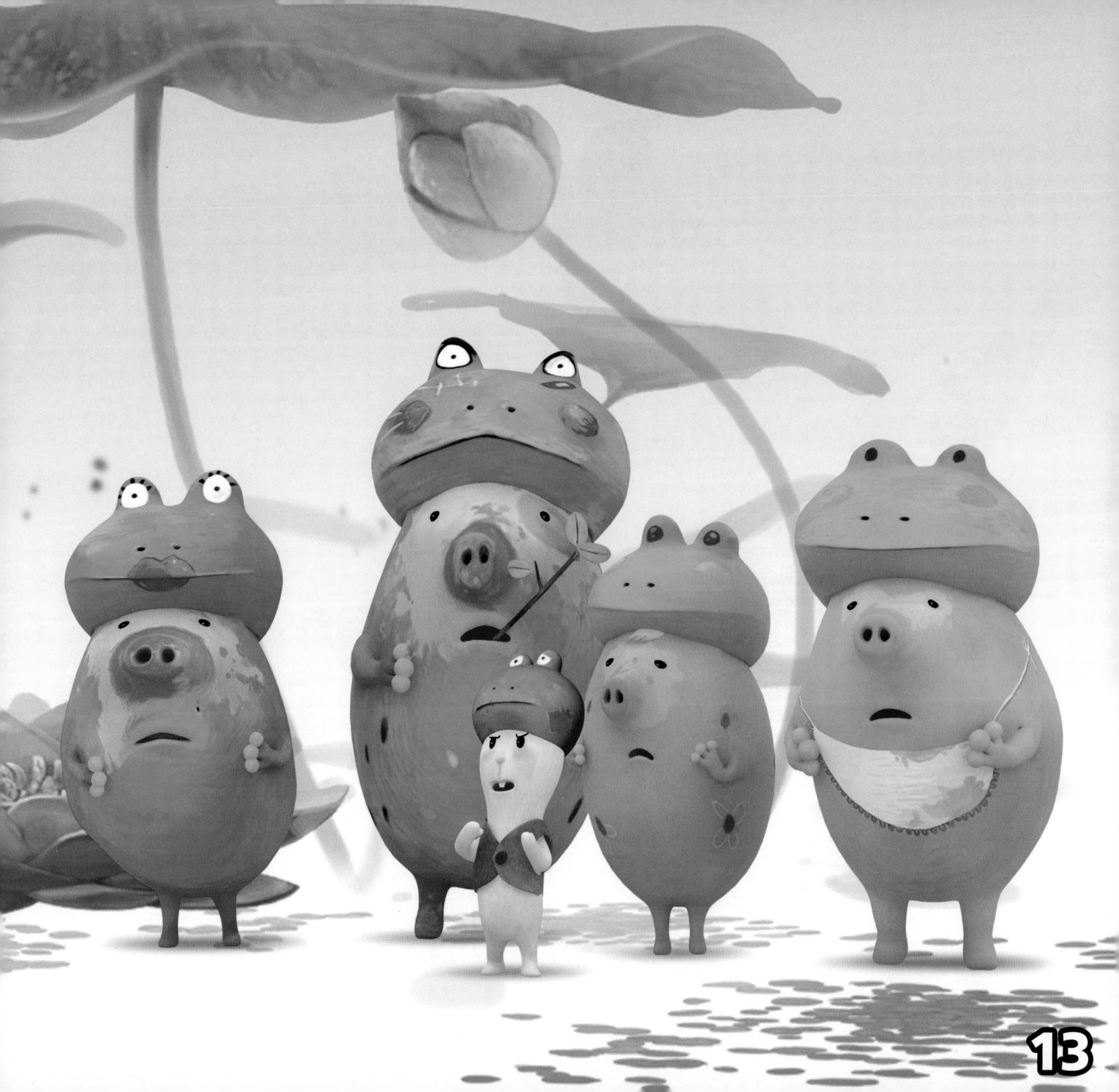

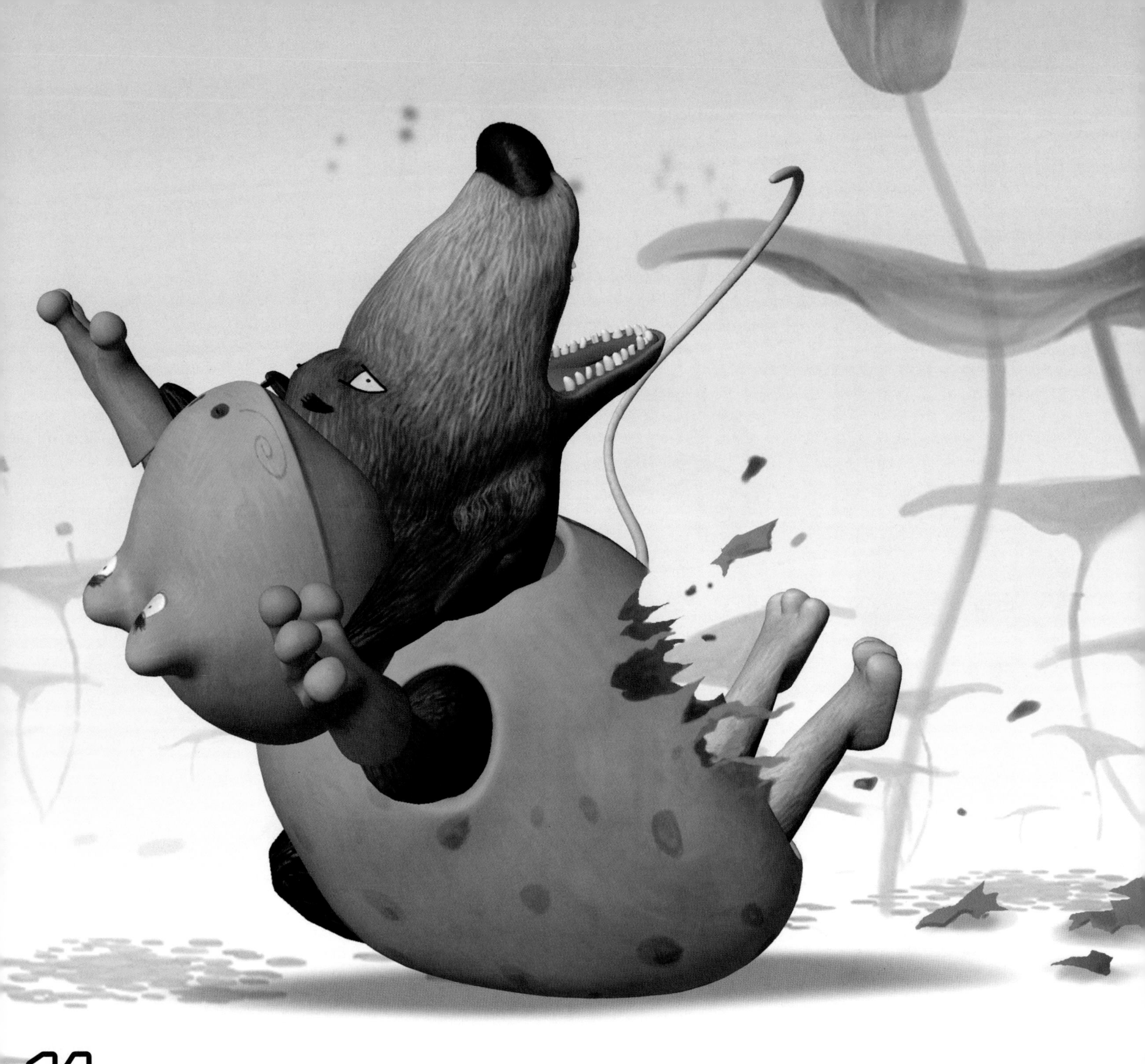

The father frog asked again.

"Was... he... bigger... than...?"

"Bang!"

The father frog burst.

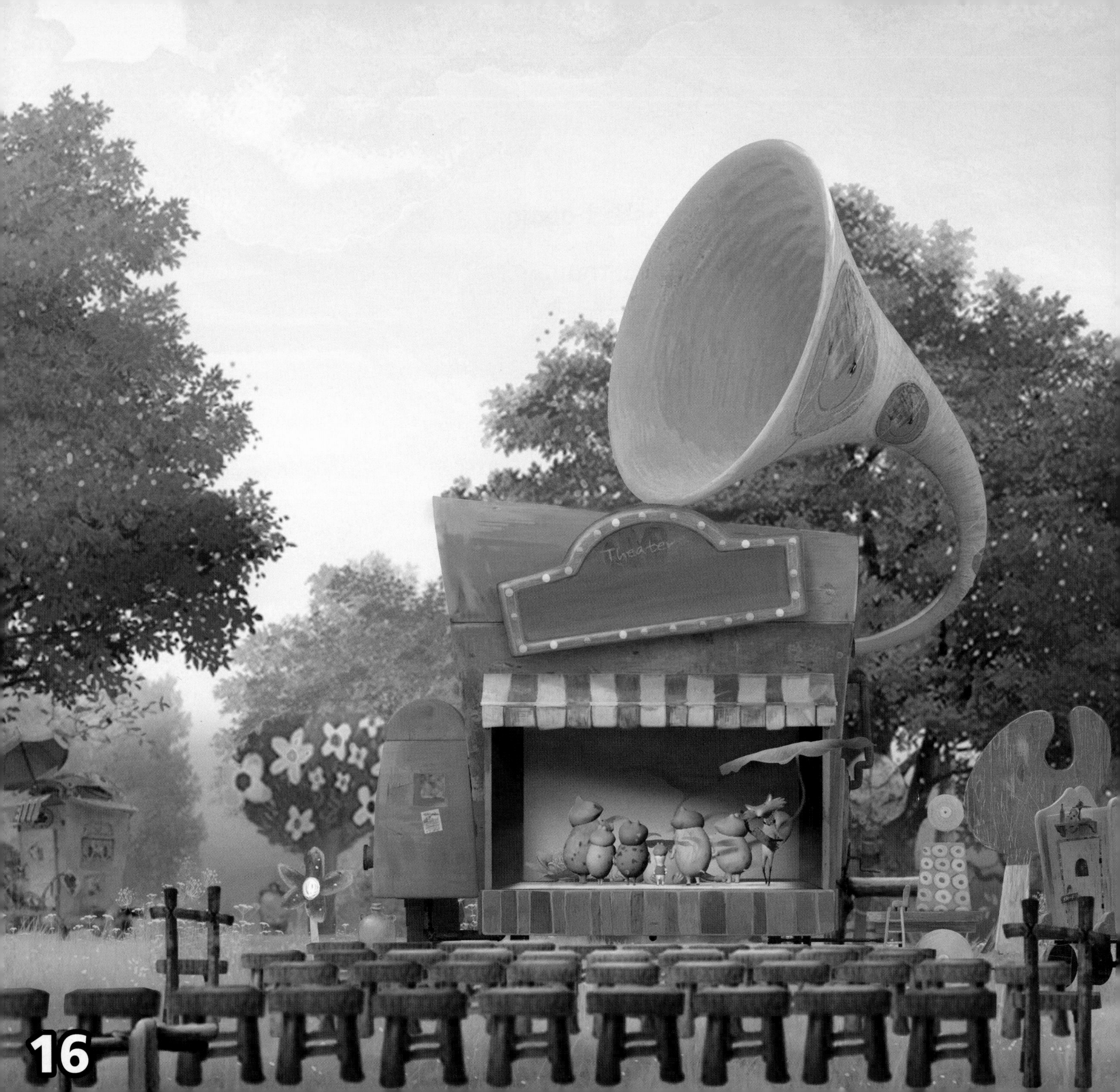
Theater

"Well done everyone!" Presy announced.

"We'll be ready for our audience tomorrow."

A mole, wandering nearby, saw a poster

blowing in the wind.

"*The Frog and the Ox*? It's a new play.

I'll tell all my friends."

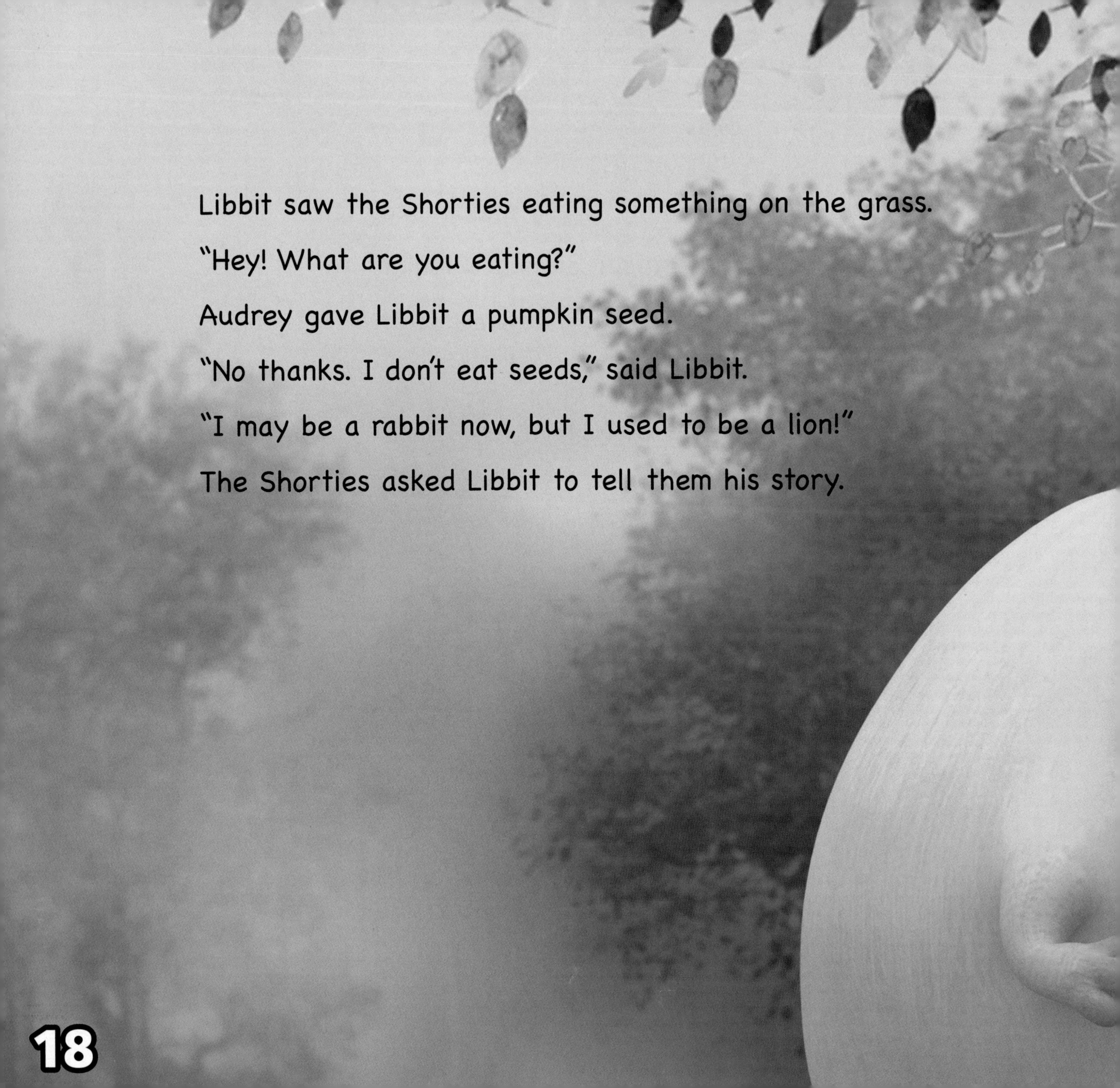

Libbit saw the Shorties eating something on the grass.

"Hey! What are you eating?"

Audrey gave Libbit a pumpkin seed.

"No thanks. I don't eat seeds," said Libbit.

"I may be a rabbit now, but I used to be a lion!"

The Shorties asked Libbit to tell them his story.

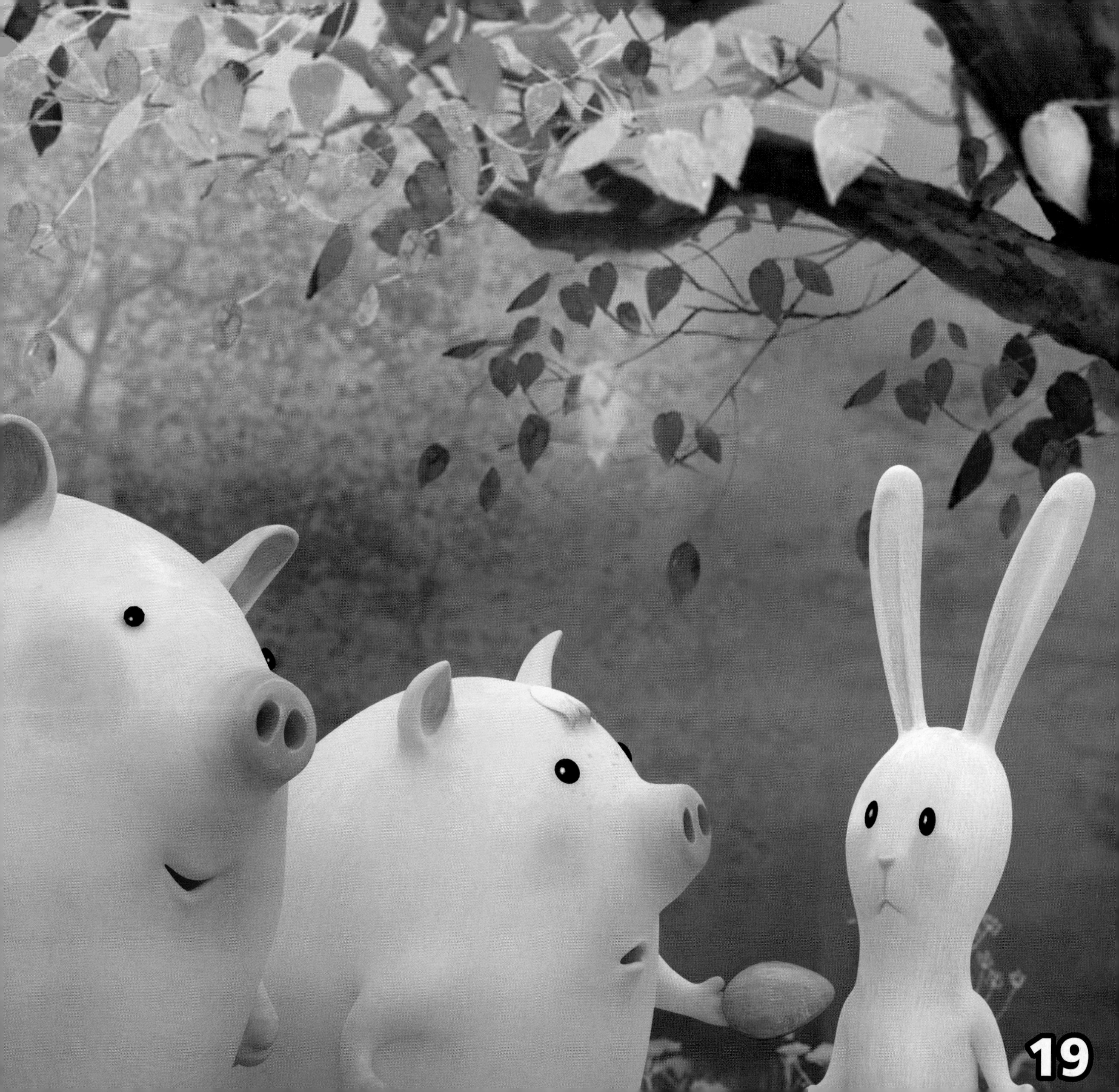

"When I used to roar," Libbit bragged,

"at least ten deer would tremble with fear.

I used to be the king of the forest!"

The Shorties looked at Libbit in wonder.

"I could take on twenty elephants."

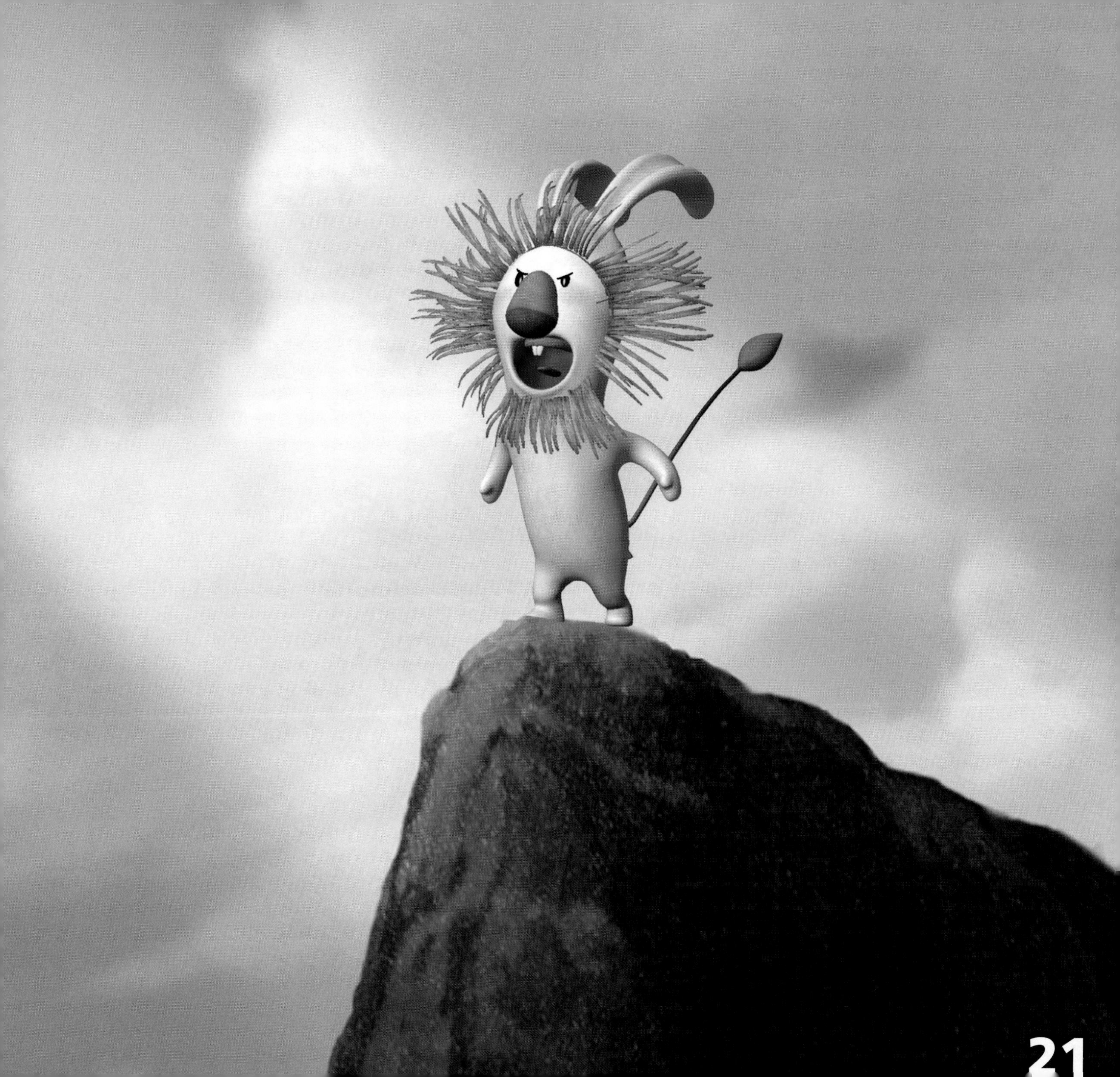

Aesop heard Libbit and said, "Dream on!"

"A weak fox doesn't know how tough lions are!" Libbit replied.

Aesop laughed loudly, "I can beat a bear!" he bragged.

"I don't believe you!" said Libbit.

"The other day, I fought a duel with a bear.

I was so strong that the bear ran away."

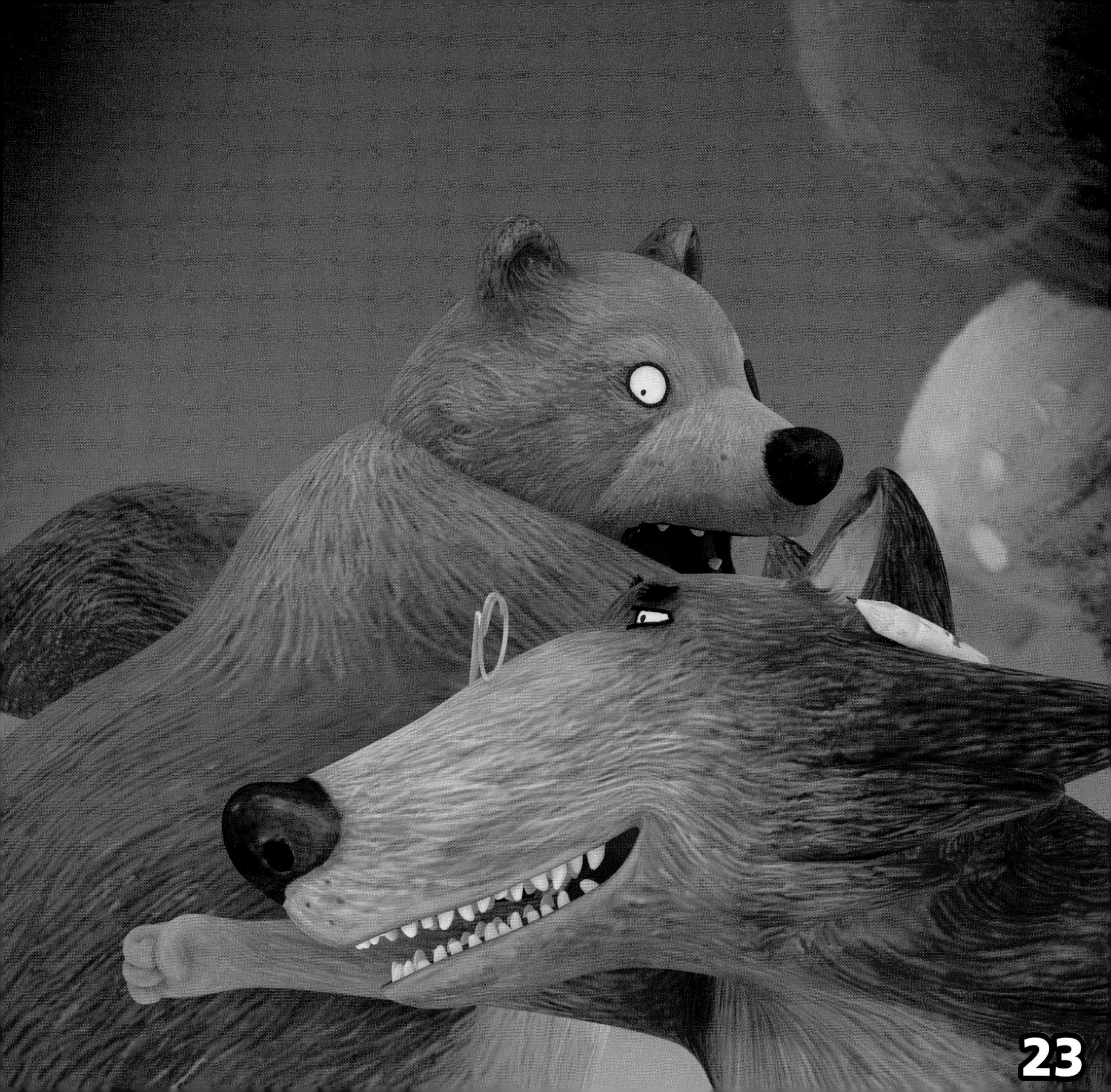

Two minutes later, a mole came to see Aesop.

"I have a message for you from the bear."

Aesop looked surprised. "What does he want?"

"The bear said that he heard you!"

"What did he hear?"

"Everything! He said he is on his way to see you."

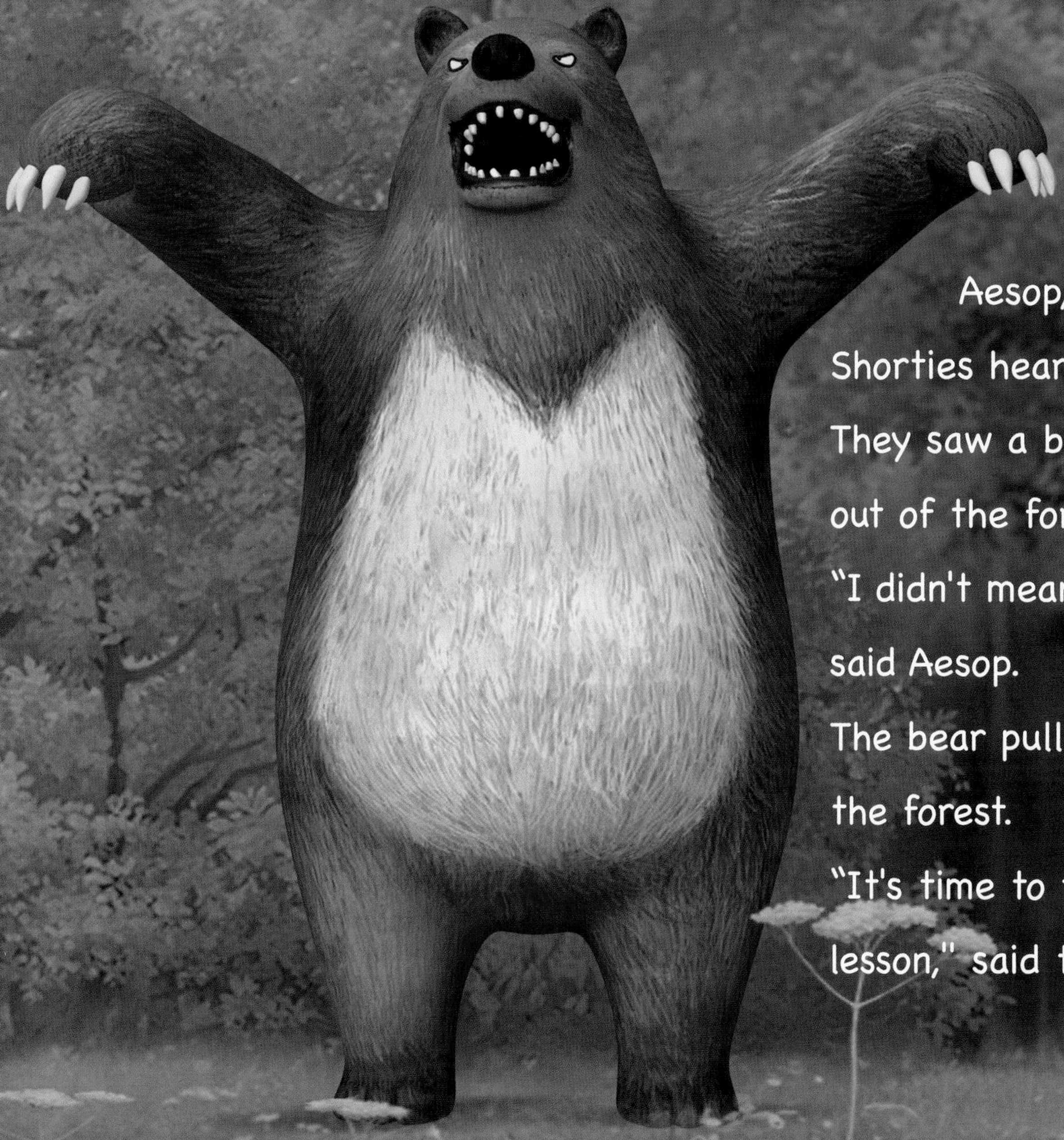

Aesop, Libbit, and the Shorties heard a loud roar. They saw a big bear come out of the forest.

"I didn't mean what I said," said Aesop.

The bear pulled Aesop into the forest.

"It's time to teach you a lesson," said the bear.

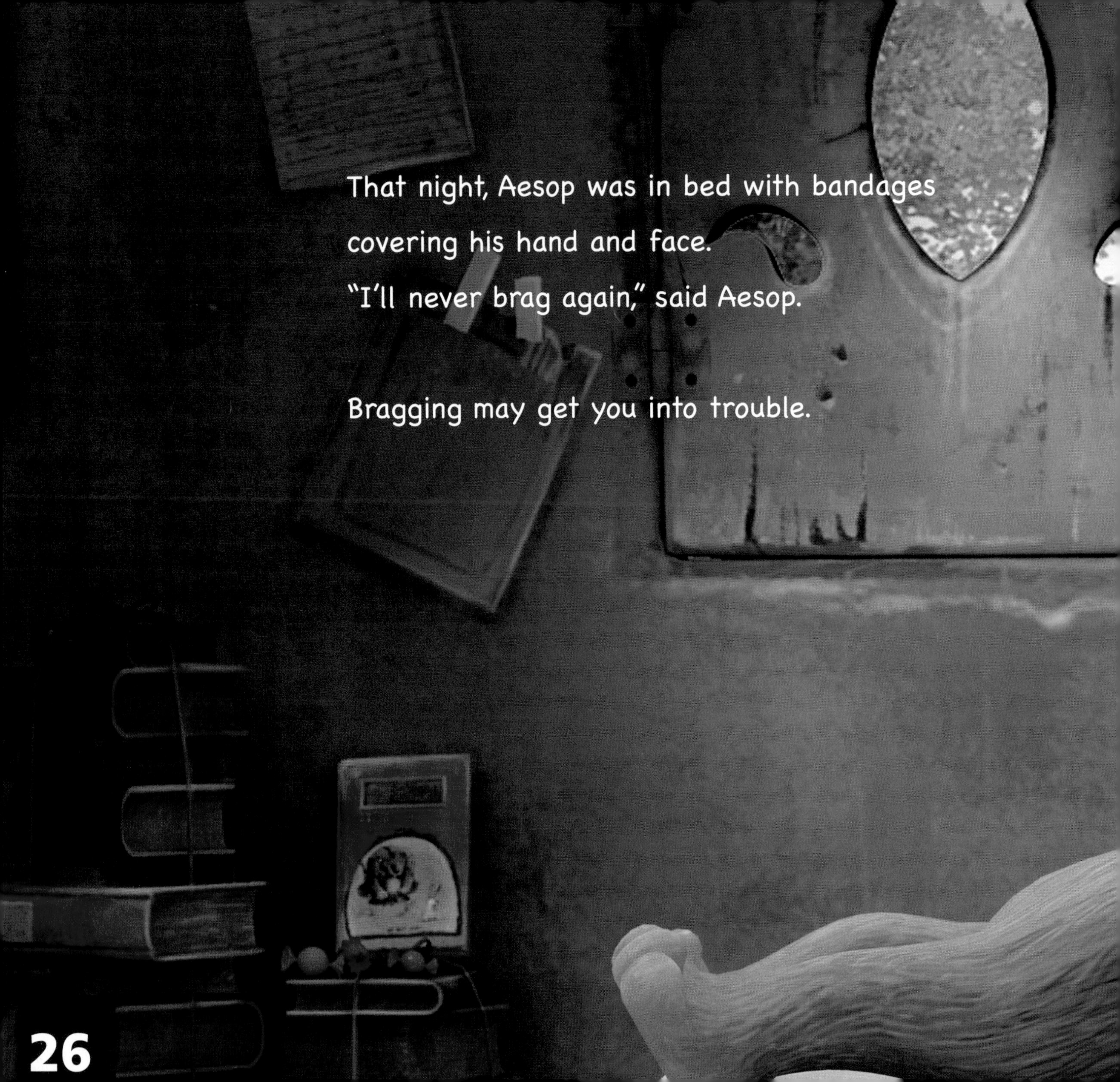

That night, Aesop was in bed with bandages covering his hand and face.

"I'll never brag again," said Aesop.

Bragging may get you into trouble.

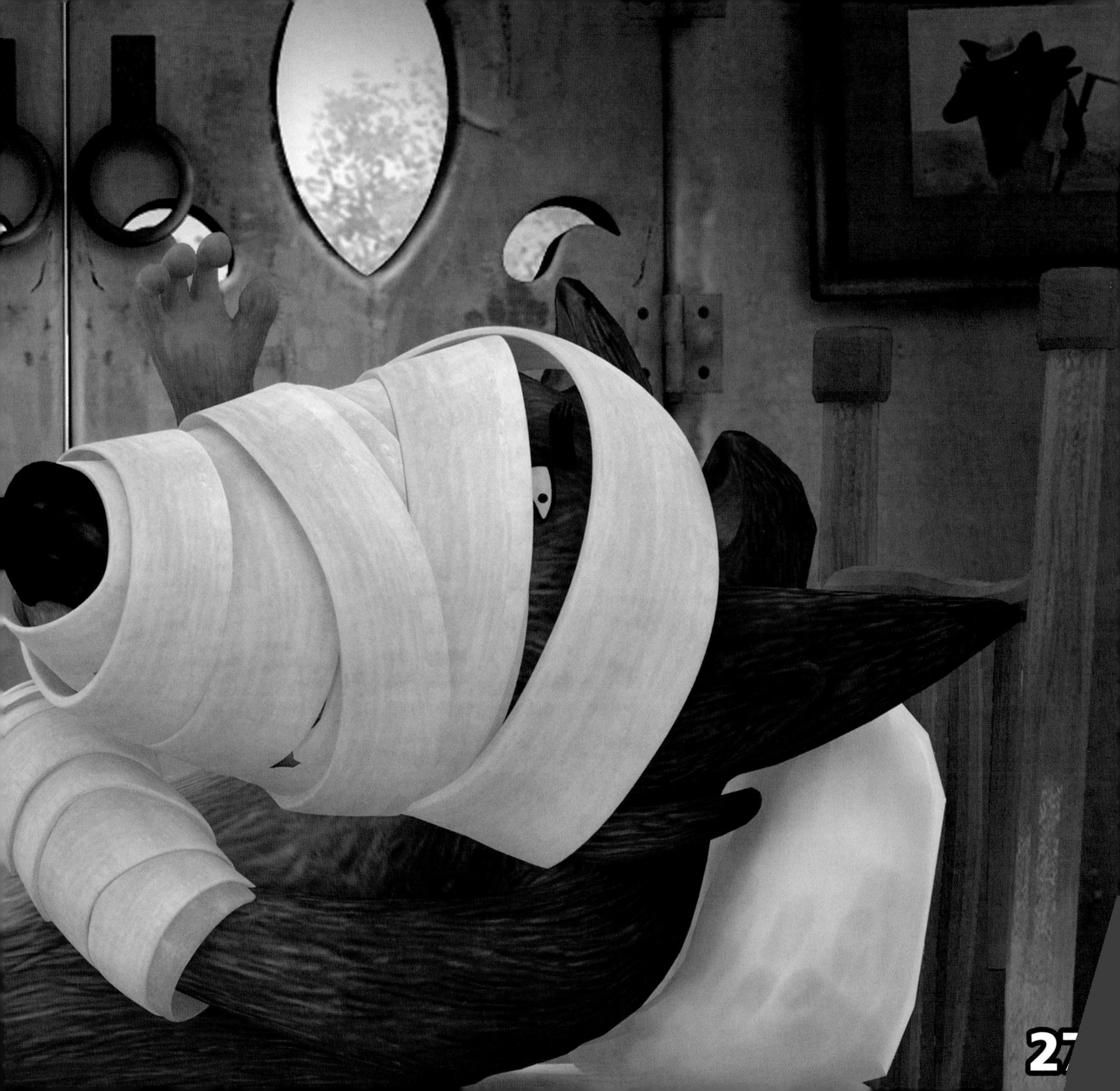

What is a Story?

Players

Who is the story about? The characters, or players, are the people, animals, or objects that perform the story. Characters have personality traits that contribute to the story. Readers understand how a character fits into the story by what the character says and does, what others say about the character, and how others treat the character.

Setting

Where and when do the events take place? The setting of a story helps readers visualize where and when the story is taking place. These details help to suggest the mood or atmosphere of the story. A setting is usually presented briefly, but it explains whether the story is taking place in the past, present, or future and in a large or small area.

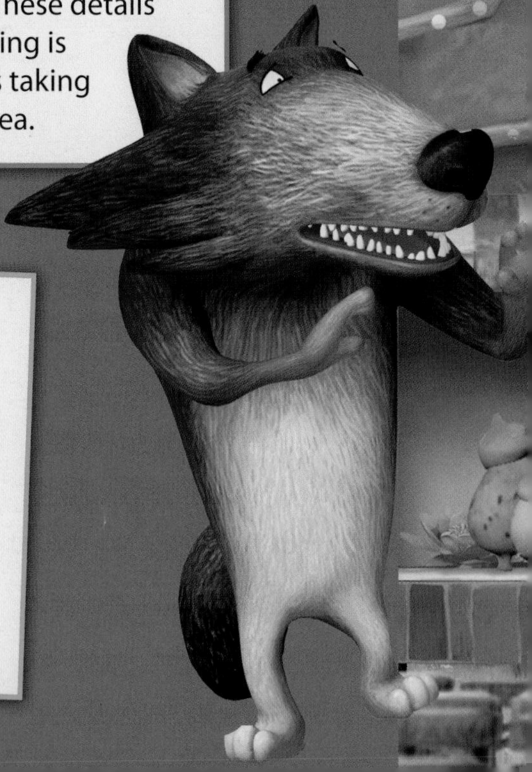

Plot

What happens in the story? The plot is a story's plan of action. Most plots follow a pattern. They begin with an introduction and progress to the rising action of events. The events lead to a climax, which is the most exciting moment in the story. The resolution is the falling action of events. This section ties up loose ends so that readers are not left with unanswered questions. The story ends with a conclusion that brings the events to a close.

Point of View

Who is telling the story? The story is normally told from the point of view of the narrator, or storyteller. The narrator can be a main character or a less important character in the story. He or she can also be someone who is not in the story but is observing the action. This observer may be impartial or someone who knows the thoughts and feelings of the characters. A story can also be told from different points of view.

Dialogue

What type of conversation occurs in the story? Conversation, or dialogue, helps to show what is happening. It also gives information about the characters. The reader can discover what kinds of people they are by the words they say and how they say them. Writers use dialogue to make stories more interesting. In dialogue, writers imitate the way real people speak, so it is written differently than the rest of the story.

Theme

What is the story's underlying meaning? The theme of a story is the topic, idea, or position that the story presents. It is often a general statement about life. Sometimes, the theme is stated clearly. Other times, it is suggested through hints.

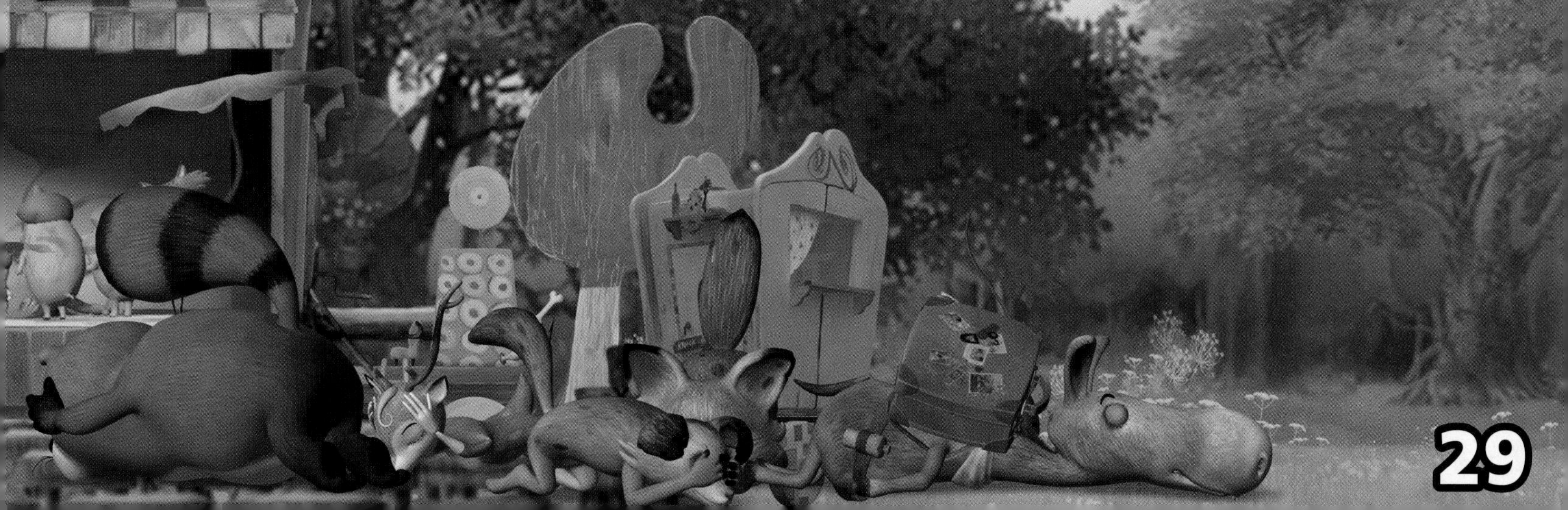

The Frog and the Ox Quiz

1
Who played the father in the play?

2
What scared the little frog?

3
Why did father frog burst?

4
What kind of seeds were the pigs eating?

5
What animal does Libbit believe he used to be?

6
What did Aesop learn about bragging?

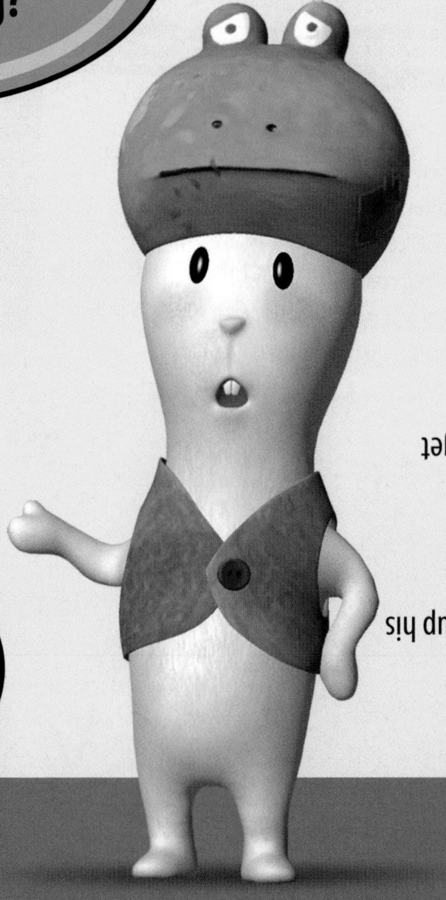

nswers:
. Aesop
. An ox
. He tried to puff up his
hest too much
. Pumpkin seeds
. A lion
. Bragging may get
ou into trouble

Key Words

Research has shown that as much as 65 percent of all written material published in English is made up of 300 words. These 300 words cannot be taught using pictures or learned by sounding them out. They must be recognized by sight. This book contains 114 common sight words to help young readers improve their reading fluency and comprehension. This book also teaches young readers several important content words, such as proper nouns. These words are paired with pictures to aid in learning and improve understanding.

Page	Sight Words First Appearance
4	a, also, am, an, and, be, been, but, can, have, I, of, plays, should, the, think, was
5	always, animals, at, do, food, from, get, good, if, like, never, other, them, to, very, want, with
6	father, large, near, one, their, were
9	before, big, had, he, head, his, just, little, long, my, not, on, out, said, saw
11	again, air, as, began, can, don't, even, into, make, me, much, now, right, then, up
12	in, last, than
15	asked
17	all, for, it's, new, our, tell, well
18	are, eat, may, no, something, story, used, what, you
20	could, take, when, would
22	away, day, how, know, so, that
24	came, did, does, hear, later, see, two, way
25	come, mean, time
26	face, hand, night

Page	Content Words First Appearance
4	actor, leader, lion, manager, narrator, prop man, rabbit, screenwriter, theater
5	dance, music, pig
6	frogs, pond
9	arms, child, daddy, horns, monster, ox, tail
11	chest
17	audience, friends, mole, poster, wind
18	grass, seed
20	deer, elephants, forest, king, roar
22	bear, fox
24	message, minutes
25	lesson, roar
26	bandages, bed, trouble

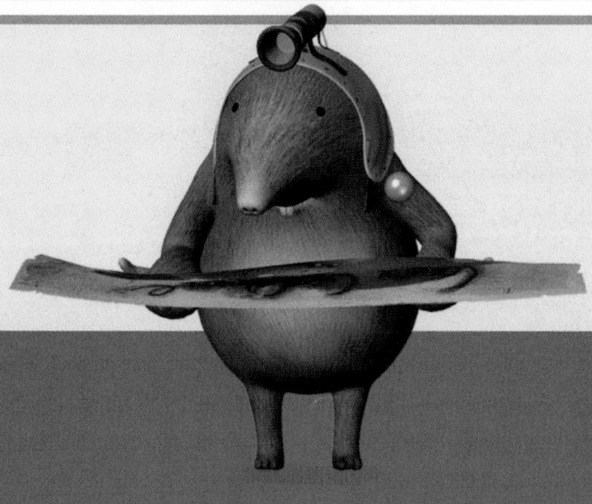

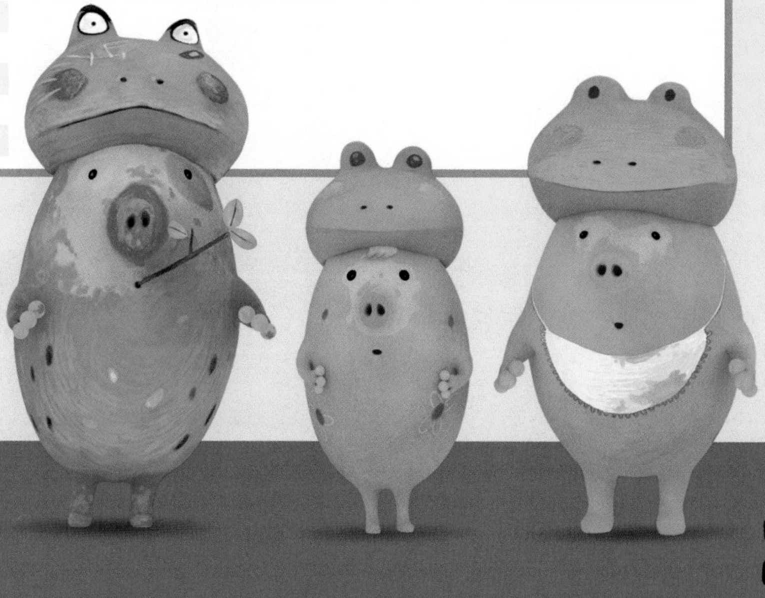

Check out av2books.com for your animated storytime media enhanced book!

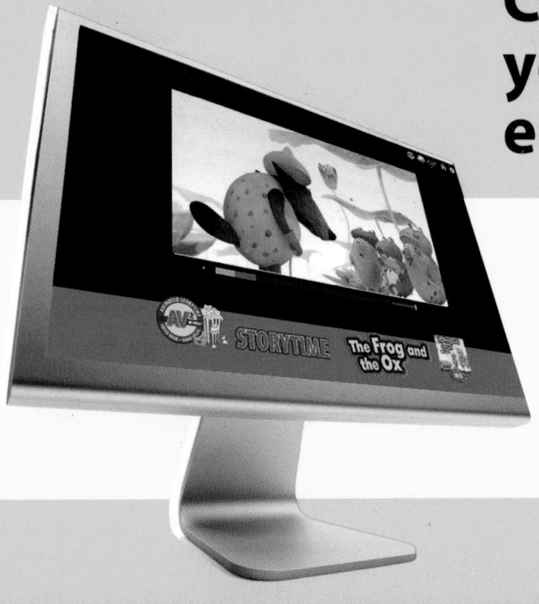
STORYTIME
The Frog and the Ox

1. Go to av2books.com
2. Enter book code **F311692**
3. Fuel your imagination online!

www.av2books.com

AV² Storytime Navigation

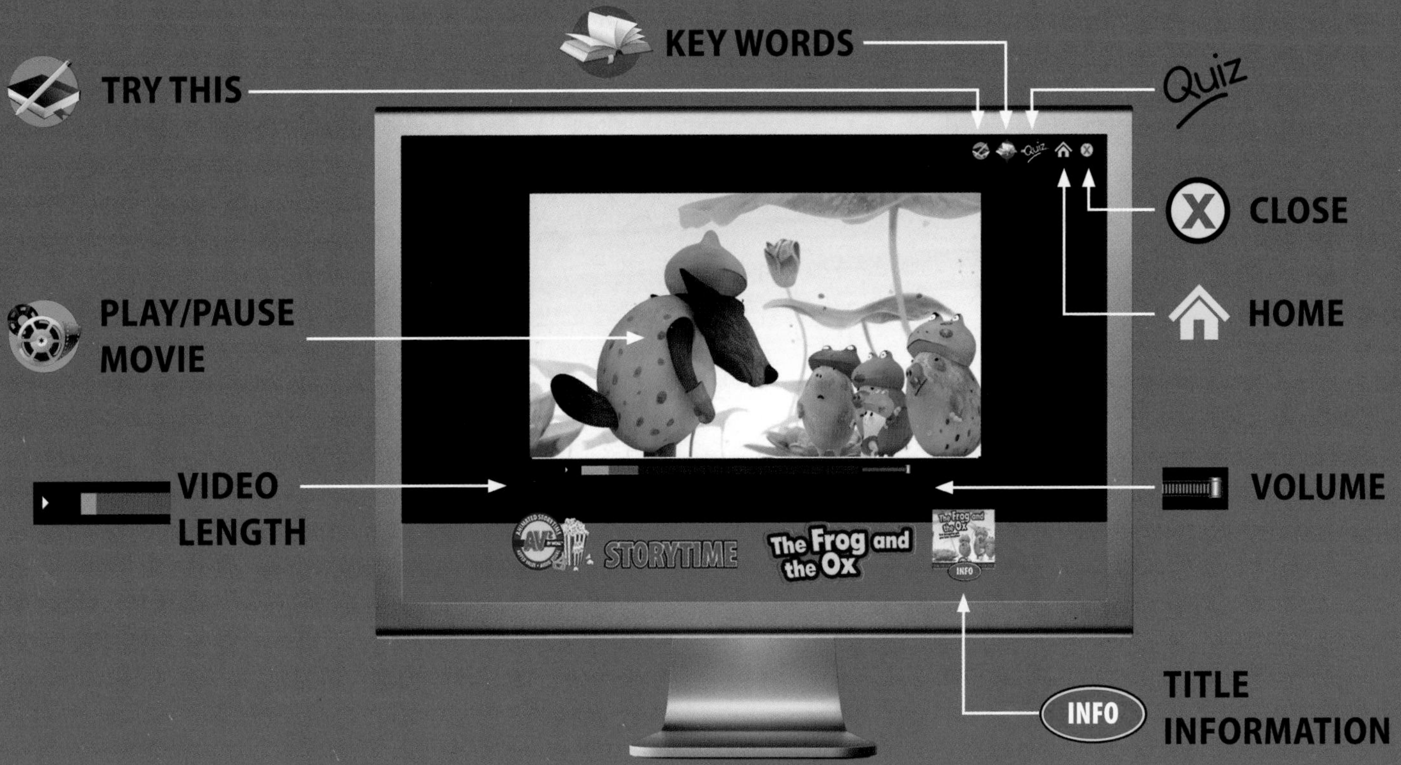
KEY WORDS
TRY THIS
Quiz
CLOSE
PLAY/PAUSE MOVIE
HOME
VIDEO LENGTH
VOLUME
STORYTIME
The Frog and the Ox
INFO
TITLE INFORMATION